DOODLE-INATOR

Printed in China

First Edition

10 9 8 7 6 5 4 3 2 1

T425-2382-5-13015

ISBN 978-1-4231-6384-8

For more Disney Press fun, visit www.disneybooks.com

Visit DisneyChannel.com

This book was printed on paper created from a sustainable source.

Based on the series created by
Dan Povenmire & Jeff "Swampy" Marsh

DISNEP PRESS

New York

Phineas found a treasure map!
Give him a crew to help him find the treasure.

Candace is on a mission to bust her brothers!
Draw the clues she's found.

Phineas and Ferb are putting on a circus. Draw the acts in their show.

What are Ferb and his friends building?

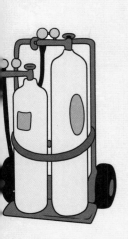

Who is Dr. Doofenshmirtz greeting?
Draw his guest to complete the scene.

Help Isabella earn her Alligator Wrestling
Patch by completing the scene.

Dr. Doofenshmirtz has trapped
Agent P with his Ballgown-inator.
Complete the scene to make
Agent P watch Doofenshmirtz's
Ballgown-inator Follies.

Phineas and Ferb built a submarine. Draw them into the scene. Where do they plan to bring their boat?

Dr. Doofenshmirtz's -inator destroyed the Great Pyramid. Add Doofenshmirtz to the scene. Draw the pyramid back in to reverse his -inator.

21

Phineas and Ferb went back in time, and now they're in trouble! Draw them on the scene. Who else is with them?

Phineas has entered a jousting match! Who is he fighting against? Draw the rest of the scene.

Baljeet built a portal to Mars.
Complete the scene to make it work.

Candace is spying on Phineas and Ferb. What does she see?

Phineas and Ferb built fighting tree-robots! Add the other robot to the scene. Who is winning the fight?

Phineas and his friends are on safari.
Add them to the scene. What do they see?

Dr. Doofenshmirtz has created a Giant Robotic Penguin Icy Freeze Your Socks Off Breath-inator Thingy. Complete the scene to show what it does.

What does Ferb's new invention do?
Add it to the scene.

Phineas and his friends are visiting an old temple. Add them to the scene. What else is happening?

Dr. Doofenshmirtz has created an Ugly-inator! Help Agent P stop him before he uses it by drawing the platypus in the scene.

Mrs. Flynn-Fletcher is building an invention of her own. What is it?

The Fireside Girls have a refreshments
stand. Add them to their booth.
What else is happening?

Phineas and Ferb built a backyard beach. Draw them on the scene. Who else is on their beach?

Dr. Doofenshmirtz is at the Inator
Creator convention. What did he create?
Who else brought -inators?

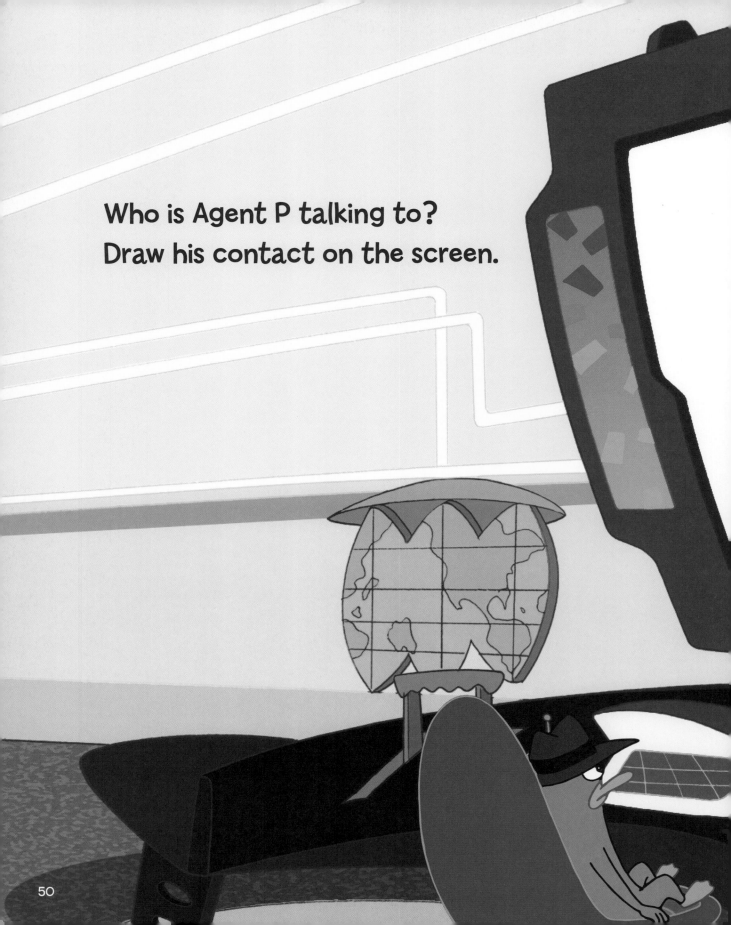

Who is Agent P talking to?
Draw his contact on the screen.

Candace and Jeremy are enjoying one of Phineas and Ferb's inventions. Where are they? Draw the rest of the scene.

The members of the O.W.C.A. are holding a secret meeting. Draw the other secret agents to complete the scene.

Dr. Doofenshmirtz and Agent P are
fighting again. Add them to the scene.
Who is winning?

56

Candace is out to bust Phineas and Ferb.
What are the brothers working on?

Dr. Doofenshmirtz has trapped Agent P. Add Doofenshmirtz to the scene. What else is happening?

Buford and Baljeet are pirates. Fill the rest of their ship with a scraggly pirate crew.

What are Phineas and Ferb building?

Phineas and Ferb have a special surprise for Candace's birthday. Add her to the scene. What else is happening?

Phineas is putting on a water show. Draw the members of his show. What are they doing?

Dr. Doofenshmirtz has a plan for the Park Your Pooch show. Add him to the scene. What did he bring with him?

Phineas and Ferb built a lemonade stand. Add Phineas to the scene. Then give them some customers.

Oh, no! Mr. Fletcher found Agent P's secret lair. Complete the scene to help the members of the O.W.C.A. erase his memory.

Dr. Doofenshmirtz has designed his own floating evil island: Doofania. What does it look like?

Phineas and Ferb are making a movie!
Add Ferb and their star to the set.

Candace and Jeremy
are on a dance show!
Add them to the scene.
Who else is dancing?

Phineas is conducting an orchestra! Draw his musicians on the page to complete the scene.

Phineas and his friends are competing in a sand castle contest. Help them complete their creation.

Dr. Doofenshmirtz created a Kick-inator.
How does it work? Draw the rest of the scene.

Phineas and Ferb made a giant dartboard! Draw the brothers and their friends on the scene to see them play their game.

Phineas and Ferb built a rodeo in the backyard! Add them to the scene to give their guests a real show!

Dr. Doofenshmirtz captured Agent P!
What is the evil doctor doing?
Draw the rest of the scene.

Phineas and Ferb created an Animal Translator. What does it do? Draw the rest of the scene.

Dr. Doofenshmirtz built a Buoyancy Operated Aquatic Transport. What does it look like? Draw it on the scene.

Phineas and Ferb are exploring underwater.
Add Ferb to the scene. What do they see?

Isabella is holding a Fireside Girls meeting. Add the other members of her troop. What are the girls doing?

Dr. Doofenshmirtz created a Mime-inator!
What does it do?

Uh-oh. Candace accidentally got transported to Mars! Add her to the scene. What is going on around her?

Phineas and his friends are visiting Baljeet's family. Add the gang to the scene.

Phineas and Ferb created a new winter sport! How did they do in the competition? Draw them into the scene.

Candace and Stacy are at the fun house. Draw them on the scene. What do their reflections look like?

Phineas and his friends are enjoying
a day at the beach. Use your
stickers to complete the scene.

116

Isabella wants to be a journalist.
Use your stickers to complete the scene.

Phineas and Ferb are building a golf course. Use your stickers to complete the scene.